In Our House

ANNE ROCKWELL

Thomas Y. Crowell New York

In Our House
Copyright © 1985 by Anne Rockwell
Printed in the U.S.A. All rights reserved.

Library of Congress Cataloging in Publication Data
Rockwell, Anne F.
  In our house.

  Summary: A member of the Bear family explores the
rooms in their house, relating all the activities that
take place there to make their house a happy home.
    1. Children's stories, American.   [1. Dwellings—
Fiction.   2. Family life—Fiction.   3. Bears—Fiction]
I. Title.
PZ7.R5943In 1985   [E]   85-47535
ISBN 0-694-00038-8
ISBN 0-690-04488-7 (lib. bdg.)

                10 9 8 7 6 5 4 3 2 1
                        First Edition

for Rocky

This is my family —
my mother, my father
and me.

This is the house
where we live.

This is our living room.
It is full of nice things.

What do we do in our living room?

feed
the
goldfish

dust
the
furniture

talk on the telephone

water the plant

vacuum
the
rug

play
the
cello

watch TV

play checkers

knit
warm sweaters

roast chestnuts

read
books

put records
on the record player

set
the
clock

open
presents

dance

change
the
light
bulb

pull
the
drapes

pay bills

milk
cocoa
bananas
potatoes

This is our kitchen.
It is full of nice things.

What do we do in our kitchen?

have breakfast

make lemonade

mop the floor

make ice cubes

throw away the garbage

read the newspaper

drink coffee

put away the groceries

set the table

cook supper

dry dishes

roll out cookie dough

clean cabinets

pull taffy
with my friend

pack a
picnic lunch

wash
dishes

cut
onions

write the grocery list

...ke greeting cards

snip
parsley

...eat eggs

look up recipes

polish
pots
and
pans

This is our basement.
It is full of nice things.

What do we do in our basement?

paint pictures

wash the clothes

fold the laundry

tie up
old newspapers

put jelly and jam
on shelves

read
the
meters

turn on
the circuit
breakers

check
the furnace

play Ping-Pong

sweep
the
floor

iron
the
clothes

This is our garage.
It is full of nice things.

What do we do in our garage?

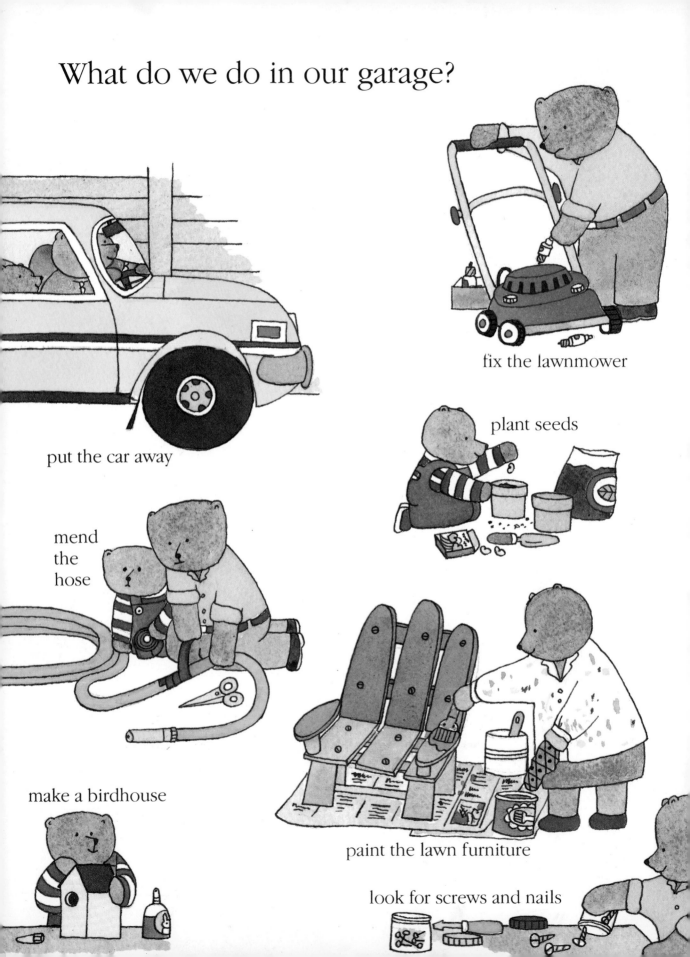

fix the lawnmower

put the car away

plant seeds

mend
the
hose

make a birdhouse

paint the lawn furniture

look for screws and nails

saw
wood

clean paintbrushes

hammer
nails

put
away
pails
and
shovels

put air in the bicycle tires

measure
things

wax
the car

put
away
the
watering
can

This is our bathroom.
It is full of nice things.

What do we do in the bathroom?

put
dirty
clothes
in the
hamper

gargle away
sore throats

clean
cuts

put on Band-Aids

get
weighed

take
a
bath

shave whiskers

sail boats

scrub
the tub

fix the drain

get dry

wash hands

go to the toilet

put on perfume

sing in
the shower

have
a
shampoo

brush teeth

This is my very own room.
It is full of nice things.

What do I do in my room?

get dressed

play with my teddy bear

build with blocks

play with my cars and trucks

make music

find lost toys

ride the rocking horse

make my bed

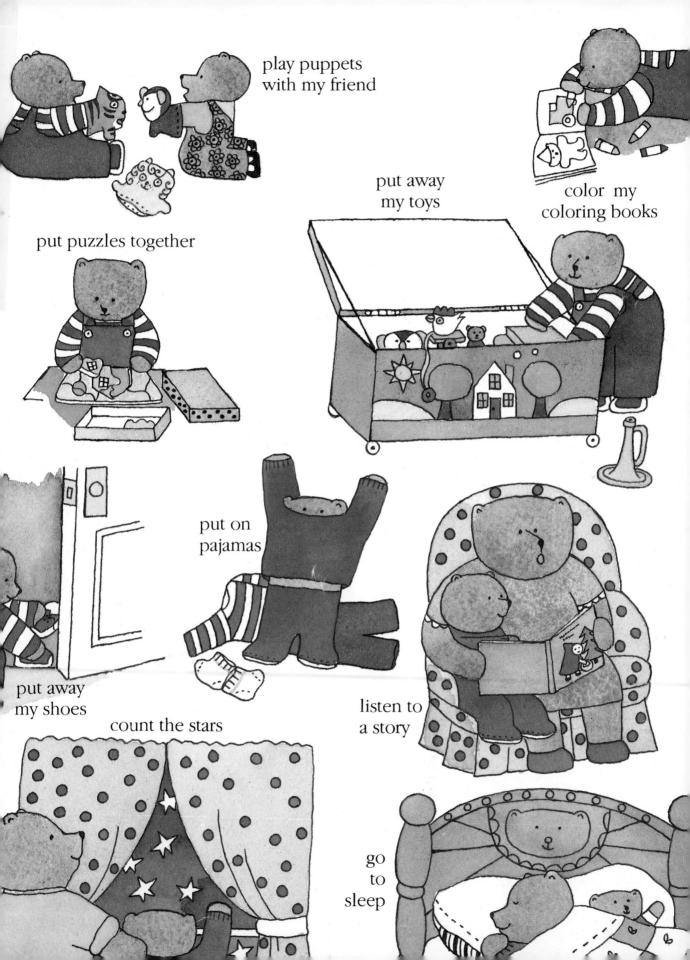

play puppets
with my friend

color my
coloring books

put away
my toys

put puzzles together

put on
pajamas

put away
my shoes

count the stars

listen to
a story

go
to
sleep

We love our house.
It is our home.